# FIGHT THE WIND

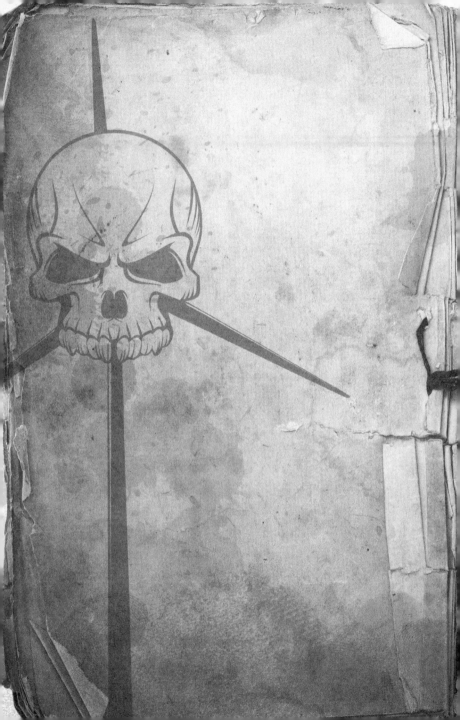

AFTER THE DUST SETTLED

# FIGHT THE WIND

ELIAS CARR

BACON ACADEMY LMC

*darbycreek*

MINNEAPOLIS

Darby Creek
A division of Lerner Publishing Group, Inc.
241 First Avenue North
Minneapolis, MN 55401 U.S.A.

Website address: www.lernerbooks.com

Cover and interior images: © iStockphoto.com/seamartini (skull); © iStockphoto.com/Diane Labombarbe (wind turbines); © iStockphoto.com/Lou Oates (antique blank album page, background); © iStockphoto.com/Anagramm, (burnt edge, background); © iStockphoto.com/Evgeny Kuklev (aged notebook background); © iStockphoto.com/kizilkayaphotos (coffee stain); © iStockphoto.com/José Luis Gutiérrez (Fingerprints); © iStockphoto.com/Bojan Stamenkovic (burnt paper background).

Main body text set in Janson Text LT Std 55 Roman 12/17.5.
Typeface provided by Adobe Systems.

Carr, Elias.
    Fight the wind / by Elias Carr.
        p. cm. — (After the dust settled)
    Summary: Seventeen-year-olds Fix, a natural mechanic, and Cleo, a gifted tactician, must find a way to cooperate in a near-future Iowa or they and the group they lead may die at the hands of armed bands rumored to be making their way down from the north.
    ISBN: 978-0-7613-8331-4 (lib.bdg. : alk. paper)
    [1. Survival—Fiction. 2. Cooperativeness—Fiction. 3. Leadership—Fiction. 4. Iowa—Fiction. 5. Science fiction.]
I. Title.
PZ7.C229323Fig 2012
[Fic]—dc23                                              2012007425

For Brother Francis

# CHAPTER ONE

The sun would be up in a few hours, so really Fix was only stealing a few hours of battery. Candles were no good. He needed light in the right places. He needed the headlamp. And if he was right, and this setup worked, a couple hours of battery would be meaningless. He and the others would have power. They'd be set. Maybe for good.

Mom and Dad would have understood. This was exactly what they died for.

Anyway, that is what Fix told himself when

he finally gave up on sleep after thrashing in bed for hours. He couldn't shake the image of the gearbox that connected the windmill to the mill's generator. He could see the way they should go together so the huge main shaft would link up with the generator again. So that it would make electricity. So he and the rest could stop running.

He couldn't shake the image. He couldn't tune out the sound of the wind and those beautiful blades spinning a hundred feet above them. The others were already sleeping, but it was a perfect night to work. And there was no way was he going to fall asleep.

When Fix got to the windmill, things immediately started to click. He was at least half right about how to get the connection back between the generator and the main shaft. There was just that one part where he wasn't so sure he remembered the words from the book. He stared at the part for the longest time, trying to recall what Cleo had said when she read the words to him earlier in the day.

Stupid words.

So Fix tightened everything down. The last thing to do was to engage the clutch that made the shaft engage the gearbox. Then the wind would turn the generator. Then they'd have power.

For a moment before he pulled the three-foot iron lever to start up the clutch, he worried that he'd wake everybody up. The lights in the bunker could easily have been switched on already. It's not like the previous owners of this farm had turned off the lights on their way out.

He decided not to worry about it. Who'd want to sleep when they had power? So he pulled the lever and felt the clutch plates grab.

Fix knew instantly that something was wrong, and he tried to push the lever to disengage the clutch. But it was too late. An ungodly screech filled the turbine walls, then the sound of snapping metal. The lever swung toward him, and a terrible pain coursed through his shoulder.

• • •

It was only a couple hours before sunrise, and Fix wasn't bothering with the flashlight. *Might as well save the battery*, he thought. Besides, in the dark he wouldn't have to know how badly he had mangled the link between the gearbox and the generator, not to mention his shoulder. How many months of work had he wrecked because he'd been impatient? Because of those stupid words.

# CHAPTER TWO

**N**o one was going to miss the two minutes of battery that Cleo would use. No one even knew she had the clippers. Of course, Fix and Todd and Rob would guess when they saw, but what were they going to say? That they had to save battery so Fix could get the stupid windmill working again?

"I ought to take my time and use the rest of this set," Cleo mumbled to herself. Fix was out of his mind. When they were out of batteries, they'd have no choice but to keep moving south. They'd all be better off.

She clicked on the smallest guard and turned on the clippers. The sooner her stupid hair was out of her way, the sooner she'd be able to think straight. *And somebody in this group has to think straight*, she thought. *Think like a soldier.* Or they'd all die. Simple as that.

It didn't even take two minutes to buzz it all off.

Clean. Uncomplicated. It felt good, like the way her head was meant to feel. Prickly under her palm.

When she finished, she left the last couple inches of candle burning while she got out her dad's book. Or what was left of his book. The cover was gone, and the first page just started in the middle of something. But that didn't matter. Lately she was pretty sure there was a message on page one just for her.

*Under my battlements. Come, you spirits*
*That tend on mortal thoughts, unsex me here,*
*And fill me from the crown to the toe top-full*

*Of direst cruelty! Make thick my blood;*
*Stop up th' access and passage to remorse,*
*That no compunctious visitings of nature*
*Shake my fell purpose, nor keep peace between*
*Th' effect and it! Come to my woman's breasts,*
*And take my milk for gall, you murd'ring*
*   ministers . . .*

She could read well enough, but some of the lines were completely meaningless to her. And yet she got the point: in war there's no place for girly girls. It was time to do something.

She dug through the bag where she'd kept the clippers hidden since she'd made the trip south from Minnesota. The tight bundle was still there at the bottom. It was still heavy. She unwrapped the cloth for the first time in days. The gun was clean.

Cleo flipped out the cylinder and spun it. The whirr was satisfying, and decisive somehow. Fix wasn't the only one who knew how to take care of a machine.

The four shells were still rubber-banded tight together. The only four shells she had—

the only four anyone had for miles, as far as she knew. *Anyone human*, she thought.

It would be six if it weren't for what they'd found when they first got to the farm. If she hadn't let Fix talk her into checking out the windmill in the first place.

# CHAPTER THREE

When sleep came and the pain in his shoulder eased, Fix dreamed of the windmill, as he always had these past few months. There were good dreams about the windmill, dreams where lights in the old house blazed and everyone inside was happy, warm, and well fed.

This wasn't the good dream. This was the memory of the first time they saw the windmill. The dream was as vivid as the moment itself.

He and the others had seen the blades rotating as they crested the off-ramp. The working windmill was the first they'd seen in days. All the rest had been mowed down like dandelions. Fix immediately wanted to check it out. Cleo had agreed, but only because she hoped they could find gas. She'd insisted that they leave the vehicle and that only she and Fix go down. Rob and Todd would stay with the kids.

Cleo pulled a bundle out of her bag in the vehicle. "If you hear me signal, head for cover."

"How are you going to signal?" Todd had asked.

Cleo unrolled the package and revealed the gun.

"Where'd you get that?" asked Rob.

"Doesn't matter. You hear me fire, you take cover in those woods. Don't come out until you get word from me or Fix. Got it?"

So Fix and Cleo walked down the valley toward the house. In his dream, they came straight up the driveway—the quick way from the highway. In reality, Cleo had made them take a wide loop around the property so they could come from the back side of the house, from near the river.

It hadn't mattered. No one had been there to greet them. The back door of the house was off, and it was clear that there'd been a fight. Recently. Cleo kept the gun out and ready.

The noise of the empty house stuck in Fix's dream. Wind blew at the curtains through the glassless window frames, and shattered plates crunched under his feet. Cleo and Fix made their way through the kitchen toward the front of the house. Everything was broken and torn open.

Cleo gestured to a wall with a hole blown through it. "Bullet hole."

Maybe it had been the wind and the noise of broken stuff underfoot, or maybe the old couple had just been quiet in their suffering.

They were near the front door. A man and a woman, barely older than Fix's parents had been. They sat propped up against each other, backs to the wall. Their dry lips mouthed the word *please*. There was blood everywhere around them, and both had clearly been shot several times.

It made no sense in this world that the couple would ever answer a knock at the front door, but that's what it looked like. As though they'd opened the doors to greet visitors together, only to be shot.

Fix froze when he saw the two, and the next few moments were like a movie he could only watch.

Cleo sprung into action. She brought the water bottle to the lips of the man—he looked the most aware. Then to the woman. The "please" got louder. Cleo whirled around and headed into the kitchen. She was back a moment later with a single filthy towel.

"Look for some rags, Fix. Anything to get this bleeding under control. Move it!" But Fix was still only a spectator.

Cleo kneeled in front of the man, trying to decide where to start. Then the woman hacked a bloody cough and pointed at the gun Cleo had shoved in her belt. "Mercy." She reached for the gun.

Cleo stumbled back, gun instantly in her hand. The man coughed too and struggled for words. "Please. You can't save us. But don't. Don't let them. Come back for us. Don't leave us for them." He pointed at the gun and then tapped the woman's forehead and his own. "Please. They'll be back. More of—" The rest was lost in coughing.

The woman seemed farther gone than the man, but his spasm of coughing seemed to snap her back to life for a moment. Her moaning stopped, and she managed to lock eyes with Cleo. Then one word: "Shelter." Her eyes rolled toward the door, and she slid farther down the wall. Then the moaning again.

Fix stayed frozen until Cleo slapped him hard across the mouth.

"Snap out of it. We've got to get back to the others. You heard what he said. This place is a deathtrap. We've got to move."

Mind working at half speed, Fix gazed through the shattered windows. He could see the windmill turning peacefully in the strong wind. The property held not just the main house, but also a large barn and several smaller buildings near the turbine. It was everything he'd hoped for.

"Fix, come on!"

Then, from the man: "Finish us. Before they come back. Please."

Fix shuddered. He looked to the man and woman and then back at Cleo. "We've got to. We can't leave them."

"We've got six bullets, and god knows how many armed monsters could be coming back any minute. You want me to waste two bullets?"

"Who's a monster if we leave these people, Clee?"

She walked away, and Fix reached for her, stumbling to catch up.

Cleo paused. He could tell she knew he was right. That had always made her madder than anything else.

"Give me the gun, Clee. I'll do it." Fix put his hand out, and Cleo stood still, the muscles of her back rippling under her T-shirt.

Without a warning or a wasted motion, Cleo spun around, knocked Fix to the ground with her left hand, fired twice, and stormed out the door. The moaning stopped.

After Fix confirmed the couple was dead, he found Cleo standing on the porch, staring into the hills. "Now can we get out of here?" she said.

# CHAPTER FOUR

$C$leo walked the hills around the farm most mornings when she couldn't fall back to sleep—if it wasn't ridiculously cold. If Rob or Todd or Fix ever asked, she would have said she was patrolling. But what was there to patrol? And what would she do if she saw anything?

Really, she liked to linger by the highway exit, the place where the truck had rolled to a stop all those months ago.

It had been hard for her to leave Minneapolis. She'd hated the cold, but she could tell something was happening in the city. The scattered collections of survivors, the little neighborhoods of the living, were beginning to organize. People were banding together. They were watching out for themselves in most cases, pooling resources and all that good stuff. But there was aggression just beneath the surface. Some groups weren't content with what they had. Some groups were looking for an advantage.

Cleo had lived with Fix and his siblings in a small house in a neighborhood with a few other inhabited houses. It was nice, and all the regular residents got along well. The neighbors weren't too friendly, although they watched out for the younger kids. It was the nicest neighborhood Cleo could imagine in this world.

But it was maybe a little too nice. Part of that was Fix's fault. Improving stuff was in his nature, and some of his projects were attracting attention. Things like a small wind turbine generator (it only worked a little, but still) and the jungle gym that Gus, Fix's little brother, loved were hard to miss among so much broken stuff.

At first it was just unfamiliar faces roaming the street. People passed through often enough, but these guys were lingering. Taking notice. Coveting.

Cleo noticed, of course. At first she thought it might be to their advantage. If they could show a few of these wanderers that they had good stuff and they weren't afraid to protect it, they might gain some allies. Cleo wasn't against sharing some of Fix's handiwork if it would expand their circle of friends a bit.

Fix, on the other hand, was completely spooked. He didn't like the fact that they had to live so close to neighbors of any kind. Unfamiliar faces set him on edge. Cleo knew this, but for a while, she thought she could manage it.

And then someone stole the new rain collector Fix had built. It wasn't just theft. It was a message. The gang that did it didn't even try to be sneaky. They just rolled up with a push truck and twenty guys Cleo and

Fix's age. They lit up the street with torches and calmly loaded up the collector. A few stood leaning against the cart, watching Cleo and Fix's front door the whole time. With the lights out, they couldn't see Cleo and Fix watching back. But the meaning was clear enough, Cleo thought. *We're taking your stuff, and you can't stop us.*

The message was so clear that Cleo was shocked when one of the guys went further. Someone threw a torch, followed by a dead squirrel, through the front window as they rolled away. The torch burned out harmlessly, and the squirrel was fresh enough that they still ate it the next day, but the damage was done. In the morning, Fix set to work on the truck. Cleo didn't try to talk him out of it. She knew they were badly outnumbered. They had only one weapon between them—and only she knew about it. And she'd noticed that none of their neighbors had shown their faces that night or the next morning. She knew her dream of an alliance was a fantasy.

A week later, they pushed off, all four of them crowded into a small pickup truck running on a sail and half a tank of diluted diesel.

And as they rolled out of the neighborhood, Fix's little sister, Nic, cried out "Look!" from her perch in the pickup's bed. Cleo and Fix twisted to see Nic's pointing hand through the broken-out rear window. Five boys—probably from the night before—were kicking in the front door.

"Vultures," Cleo spat and turned toward the road ahead. *No sense in looking back any more*, she thought.

"The door wasn't even locked," whispered Nic. Cleo could hear the two younger kids whispering to each other in the back, trying to be brave for each other.

"It'll be warm wherever we end up."

"Yeah, and lots of food."

"And other kids."

If they could be optimistic, she decided she could be too.

The wind was good the first few days, and they made excellent progress down Interstate 35.

Cleo was beginning to enjoy the idea of putting the cold behind her. Her hope of a bigger, stronger group even got a boost when they met Todd and Rob, camping just north of the old Iowa border.

The two were shivering together in a ratty one-person tent. They'd been exiled for something Cleo and Fix couldn't quite understand from one of the communities to the east in old Wisconsin. They were quiet, but Cleo could see that they were strong. They had some of their own food, and Cleo was quick to admit that she and Fix could use the help.

So the cozy four become a cramped six, but everyone was optimistic. The wind was even good for a couple more days as they crossed out of Minnesota.

But in Iowa all their luck changed. First the wind died. And then a few stupid hills. And soon they were out of fuel.

• • •

Cleo stared down from the top of the overpass at the windmill and old house. She felt the same worried feeling in the pit of her stomach that she'd had all those months ago, when she'd looked down at the calmly spinning turbine and known something was wrong.

"Stop it," she said to herself, willing the memory away. But it wouldn't stay gone.

She'd known at the same time as Fix that they couldn't leave the old couple. Even if she'd tried to, had said she would, she knew she couldn't have. She'd also known that Fix couldn't do what needed to be done—or that if he did, it would ruin him forever. So she'd made him follow her away a little ways. And then she'd done it quickly, so neither of them would have to look the man and the woman in the eyes. It had been a risk. She might have missed. If there was any satisfaction in the memory of that bloody moment, it was in knowing that her aim had been true. And deadly. There was always that.

The aftermath was a frustrating blur. It was almost more unpleasant for Cleo to remember than the shooting. There had been no good choices. To the south, there were low, rolling hills for as far as the eye could see. It didn't take a tactical genius to see how vulnerable they would be on the road in their tiny truck.

Todd and Rob were hustling the kids out of the truck when Cleo and Fix reached it, panting.

"The woods, we can hide out there until—" Cleo whirled around, scanning the woods on the other side of the highway. The view wasn't promising. The trees were thin and quickly gave way to acres of barren farm fields. "Whoever did that—whoever did that down there will be back. And we can't be here." Her mind raced as she felt the responsibility of getting the others to safety.

"Cleo!" It was Todd. "You don't have to do this on your own. We've got time to figure this out. What happened?"

Rob and Todd each put a hand on her shoulders. Fix, who was just catching his breath, nodded. "There's got to be a place to hide out for a bit. Where we can make a plan."

Todd and Rob hadn't spoken much since they'd joined up. They'd just pitched in and become silent but strong parts of the group. Cleo was never so glad for their voices as she was then.

"Let's get what we need to camp for a few days. We'll hide the truck as best we can, and we can come back for it when it looks like we're all clear," declared Rob. Cleo could hear him trying to sound confident, but she doubted the plan. They had no useful shelter or the right gear for camping away from the truck for even a night. "We can walk north for a bit. I think there was a real forest a mile or so ago. Or maybe we'll find an old—"

"No, we've got to go back down to the farm. To the windmill." It was Fix. He'd been staring down toward the farmhouse.

Cleo had assumed he was still in shock, but now she knew she'd mistaken shock for concentration. That vacant look. He'd thought of something, and she wasn't sure she wanted to hear it.

# CHAPTER FIVE

It was rare that Fix's dream got all the way to the fire, but he'd been exhausted and this time the dream's grip was firm.

The fire had been a concession to Cleo. Fix had convinced the others that there must be some kind of shelter near the farmhouse— something like the structure Fix had a vague memory of, from before his parents died. That had been what the woman had been trying to tell them.

So all six of them raced back to the farm and searched the grounds. Nothing. And night was coming.

"We can't stay here, Fix. It's too exposed." Cleo's face was grim in the fading daylight.

Then came the sounds of oil barrels rolling and Todd and Nic calling, "A door! There's a door in the ground."

Beyond the door, they'd found the bunker. It was stocked with food and supplies. Even though it was clearly intended for two people, it was more comfortable for the six of them than the truck had ever been.

Inside the bunker, Fix had relaxed a little for the first time in a long time. He felt like he was home. Home . . .

But then there was the fire. Once they'd sorted out the bunker, Cleo decided to sacrifice a gas lamp and few fuel cylinders to "send a message to whoever attacked those people."

"If we burn down that old house, this place will look a little less welcoming. Might attract less attention," she declared.

While she rigged up the place to burn, Fix

and Todd got everything the raiders had left behind and took it to the bunker.

Fix was standing by the bunker's entrance when Cleo lit a kerosene-soaked rag and threw it through the farmhouse door. She never looked back as it burned. Fix couldn't tear his eyes away.

• • •

"Fix? Fix?" Todd's worried face was hanging over him. Fix squinted at the sunrise over Todd's shoulder, feeling tireder than ever. "You and Cleo weren't in your bunks . . . Rob stayed with the kids . . . I thought I'd find you here. Dunno about Cleo."

Fix tried to push himself up from where he'd slumped down against the wall, but his shoulder screamed with pain. He gasped and rolled onto his good side.

"Fix? What's wrong?" Todd reached out a hand to help him. Fix grabbed it and pulled himself upright.

"I did something to my shoulder," Fix mumbled, rubbing his hand across it cautiously. "When I—I was trying to fix the windmill. Almost had it. Thought I

remembered the last part of the directions
Cleo read. But I messed it up. Broke it. Didn't
remember the words right." Fix stopped, a
lump in his throat, his shoulder throbbing.

Todd reached out a hand again, pulled it
back a little, then carefully patted Fix on his
good shoulder.

"But you'll fix it, right? You always figure
this stuff out," Todd said.

Fix swallowed hard. He had been so
close . . . He wasn't stopping now. He clenched
his fist.

"Yeah, we'll fix it. We've gotten all the
stuff we can around here, but I'll find what I
need somewhere else. As soon as I see how bad
it is"—the lump came back, and he swallowed
again—"then I'll know what I need. I don't
care how long it takes to find the hardware. I'll
get it right this time. I'll get it right . . ."

Todd nodded silently.

"This place will be perfect!" Fix burst out.
"As soon as I get it working. Reminds me . . ."

Todd waited. "Of what?" he finally said.

"Of home . . ." Fix whispered.

# CHAPTER SIX

Stopping just outside the doorway, Cleo clenched her fists at Fix's words. *Home*—they didn't talk about home or their lives before or what they'd lost. Looking back only made you weaker, in her opinion. Home . . . Cleo shook her head, missing for a moment the expected tap of her braids on her face. Then she remembered why she'd buzzed her hair in the first place. She was sick of being scared. She was a warrior now.

Yes, being warrior meant you weren't

afraid to kill, but it didn't mean seeking out fights. Especially when your weapons were limited. Cleo grimaced, thinking about the last time Fix had insisted they go look for parts for that stupid windmill.

They'd left the kids with Todd and Robb at the farm. Cleo and Fix hiked across several fields toward something on the horizon that Fix swore was another farm. Cleo complained the whole way about how risky this raid was when they had plenty of food back at their own farm. She'd kept up her complaining, even as Fix stayed quiet, because she hated the creepy feeling up her spine that being exposed in the fields gave her.

When they'd finally reached the other farm, before Cleo could check to see if it was safe, Fix tried to rush into a shed filled with machinery. Cleo ripped Fix's shirt trying to hold him back and not make a lot of noise.

"Ow!" Fix had said, yanking his arm away from her. Cleo silenced him with a glare. She wished she could scream at him and smack him around for being so stupid on top of making them come there in the first place. She took a deep breath to center herself. Holding the gun at the ready, she walked slowly toward the shed, her eyes scanning the grounds. Fix hovered behind her as she entered the shed and peered around. She didn't see any place someone could be hiding.

"There's no one here," Fix muttered, shouldering past her and opening one of the machines. He let a piece of metal clank to the ground.

"Would you shut up and hurry?!" Cleo hissed. "I'll stand guard, but I'm leaving in three minutes whether you're ready or not." They both knew this wasn't true, but the place was freaking Cleo out. No telling who was in the house or those other buildings. They could hear doors squeaking in the breeze.

"Beautiful!" Fix murmured. "I don't think anyone's been in here since—"

Cleo was sure she heard a noise behind the shed. She shifted her stance, training the gun on the corner.

"Cleo!" Fix screamed. Cleo ducked and spun just in time to see a plank crashing past her shoulder. Seeing movement out of the corner of her eye, she turned again. This kid wasn't armed. As he grabbed for her, she hit him hard in the face with the gun. The first guy was raising the board again, and Cleo kicked him in the stomach. She jumped aside as the plank crashed down again as he doubled over.

*The gun*, she thought. Why weren't they afraid she'd shoot them? She hadn't, of course, because she had so few bullets left. Her mind reeled. Were there a lot of kids out here waving around guns with no ammunition? Wasn't she four shots away from becoming one of them?

Cleo watched as both the kids rolled on the ground. There was something about them that looked wrong. *Love to shoot them both*, she thought. Then she saw Fix in the doorway, holding a heavy wrench.

"Good idea," she said and grabbed it from him. She pulled her arm back, ready to brain the first guy.

"Cleo, no!" Fix yelled. They struggled for a moment before Fix yanked the wrench from Cleo's sweaty hand. "They're just kids! Younger than us—"

"They tried to kill me!" Cleo screamed, kicking one of the kids in the ribs as he tried to stand up.

A yell nearby shook them both. Three or four other kids were running toward them from one of the buildings, waving pitchforks. With their teeth bared, the kids didn't look human.

"C'mon!" said Fix, grabbing Cleo's arm and pulling her away. Cleo tried for one last kick but missed. They ran toward the patchy grove of trees across the field.

Looking back over their shoulders, they didn't see anyone following them. Still, Cleo made them take a long way back. She refused to speak to Fix—when he showed her the machine parts he'd stuffed in his backpack, she only snorted in disgust.

• • •

Cleo snorted again outside the doorway, thinking about the risks they'd taken for Fix to work on this idiotic windmill. And now it was all for nothing anyway. Not that she'd ever thought it would work out.

"We've stayed here long enough," Cleo announced, walking into the windmill shed. Todd's head snapped toward her. Fix just kept rubbing his shoulder and wincing. "We need to keep moving. We need to get where there are other people, people who are organized. I could have gotten us in with a gang in Minneapolis. I can do it in another city; we have things to offer. But we can't stay here."

Todd turned to Fix, his forehead wrinkled. Fix didn't say anything, didn't look at Cleo.

"We're sitting ducks," Cleo went on, even louder. "You saw those kids at the other farm, Fix. They were practically savages. It's just dangerous drifters out here, and sooner or later someone's going to come along who has better weapons and that will be it."

Still not looking at her, Fix managed to stand up and stumble out the door.

"You know I'm right!" Cleo yelled after him. "And I wasn't done talking! Fix!"

## CHAPTER SEVEN

Fix kicked the bunker door and heard frightened squeaks inside.

"It's just me!" he yelled.

Nic opened the door. "What's wrong?" she asked, seeing Fix holding his shoulder.

"Broke the windmill, busted my shoulder. 'S alright," he said.

Nic looked closely at her brother's face. "I know I saw some bandages and stuff in the first aid box that might help." She started rummaging.

Cleo yanked open the door. Todd came in on her heels, looking scared. Before Cleo could open her mouth, Nic turned to her and said tersely, "Save it. Let's deal with Fix's shoulder first."

Cleo scowled, surprised. She turned away to her own corner and started messing with her stuff.

Fix felt the same surprise and gratitude he'd been feeling more often toward Nic. She was still his little sister, but lately she'd seemed older. It especially helped when she did the talking with Cleo. He and Cleo were supposed to be in charge, but he never knew what to do with all the words Cleo threw at him.

Fix relaxed a little now that he was in the bunker. It was the perfect place for them to live, he thought. His parents had built one like it a few months before—

Fix gritted his teeth as Nic started trying to tie a bunch of pieces of cloth into a sling around his shoulder. He couldn't figure out how she thought this would help, but he wasn't ready for Cleo yet. So he just sat and looked around while Nic fussed over him.

The shelter was impossible to break into, Fix was sure. That's why he wasn't too worried about those other kids out there. The rainwater collection system was in perfect condition, and the shelves had enough packaged meals to last a long time. Plus they could grow stuff next year. Fix had seeds.

Fix's eyes lingered on his favorite thing about the bunker: the electrical wires. When they'd first arrived, he'd raised the low fuel level of the diesel generator by dropping rocks in the tank and managed to eke out some power. Now they needed the windmill if they hoped to have electricity. It wasn't strictly necessary, but it would make life a lot easier.

Nic stepped away from Fix, surveying her work. The sling did support his shoulder a little.

"Thanks," Fix murmured. Cleo twitched impatiently in her corner. Fix sighed. He knew Cleo hated the bunker as much as he liked it. A few times they had shut themselves in because they thought someone was prowling around their farm. Each time Cleo was in a funk for a week afterward, biting off everyone's heads.

Watching Cleo out of the corner of his eye, Fix realized that her hair was gone except for a layer of fuzz. What the—

"Where's your hair, Cleo?" Gus asked, mirroring Fix's thoughts.

"And where were you this morning?" demanded Nic.

# CHAPTER EIGHT

For a moment, Cleo blinked and ran her hand over her head. Then she shrugged.

"The hair was in my way," she muttered. Then she looked at Nic, standing next to Fix who was staring at the floor. "I'll tell you what I wasn't doing," Cleo hissed. "I wasn't wasting time and battery power working on a hopeless windmill. I wasn't getting myself hurt so I was useless. I wasn't moaning about staying here to be sitting ducks for the big gang headed our way."

"What are you talking about?" Nic said sharply. "What gang?"

"I was up on the ridge," Cleo said, starting to pace. "Patrolling. I could see smoke from their fires and see them moving around. At least fifteen of them, about a mile away."

Rob and Todd both got up and started their tasks for securing the bunker. Gus inched over next to Fix.

"And I heard gunshots," Cleo said, staring at Fix. Todd and Rob both stopped and looked at them. No one said anything.

Finally Fix turned to Cleo and said, "What do you think that means, Cleo?"

She glared at him. "Obviously they're either shooting each other or shooting other people. Or, better yet, shooting game to eat. I know they're loaded with ammunition."

"Cleo, are you going to check the camouflage on the water system or not?" Nic asked, her hands on her hips. "You guys can talk more when everything's done."

Cleo stared over Fix's shoulder as though Nic hadn't spoken. "I'm sick of this," she said softly but clearly.

Fix hadn't taken his eyes off her. "What do you want to do, Cleo?" he said.

Cleo looked down at Fix again. She looked almost sad now. "You know exactly what I want to do, Fix."

# CHAPTER NINE

Nightmare scenes of blood and twisted bodies filled Fix's head. He did know what Cleo wanted. When she had told him a while ago, that was when he started to be afraid of her. And for her. She was changing.

There was an old well in the farmyard. They used it for water when they weren't stuck hiding in the bunker. Every time after they'd hidden in the bunker because a group was coming through, Cleo had pointed out all the tracks around the well. No one could afford to ignore a water source. Some groups had hung around the farm for days, probably because of the well water.

They'd tried camouflaging the well, but the last two groups had found it anyway. Cleo said word was spreading about this farm. Fix didn't get how that was happening—he couldn't see any of the groups cooperating—but he couldn't explain it otherwise.

"It's just a matter of time before someone finds the bunker and figures out a way to get in. They could put explosives down the water-collection pipe. They could poison our water with a dead animal, or with frickin' poop for that matter. And where will we be then, Fix? Trapped like rats in a cage, waiting to be picked off one by one."

Cleo had been cleaning her gun as she spoke. She waved it in Fix's face to get his attention. He had a feeling he didn't want to hear her plan, whenever she was going to get around to it.

"And it may not have occurred to you, being so lucky as to be a guy, but someone might decide, once they'd pried open the doors of the bunker, that rather than killing me or Nic, they want something else from us. Wouldn't take more than two guys to hold Nic—"

"Stop it!" Fix had yelled, feeling sick. "What do you want?"

After Cleo explained, Fix felt sicker. How was Cleo able to twist his dreams of all of them living safely on the farm into a choice between endangering his sister and killing a lot of people?

This is what Cleo wanted. Fix would make a bunch of traps. The ones around the well would freak the rest of the nomads into running into the other traps in the farmyard, maybe even in the barn, because it would look like a safe place to run to.

Fix regretted any enthusiasm he'd ever shown for the rusty old traps they'd found in the barn. He regretted fixing them, even though they had come in handy. Even though he'd filled his belly with rabbit many times, it wasn't worth it. He knew they'd planted the seed of an idea for Cleo.

Cleo would hide in the ruins of the farmhouse, where she'd have a clear shot at anyone not caught in a trap. She figured that between those killed by traps and those she'd take out with the bullets, she'd get enough of the raiders to collect some more weapons and ammo.

"But you only have four bullets left, right?" Fix had said.

"Exactly why we need to find a way to get more, Fix!" Cleo had yelled. "Unless you have some magic bullet seeds that you plan to plant—"

Fix turned away from her, his head swimming. What would they do with the people stuck in the traps? What about the ones who ran away? Why couldn't they just keep hiding when they needed to and enjoy their new home when the groups had moved on?

"If we can gather up enough supplies, we'll be able to leave here and no one will mess with us as we keep heading south," Cleo had said coldly. "There's nothing for us here, Fix."

*Everything's here*, thought Fix.

# CHAPTER TEN

Cleo hadn't told Fix that there was another part to her plan. She was sure that once their little group was well armed, they'd be able to join another organized group as they moved south. A good show of force and anyone would see that they'd be assets. Then, when they made it to a city, they'd come in strong and be safe right away.

As everyone started to rush around, doing their jobs to secure the bunker, Cleo stalked outside. She checked the water-collection pipe and their other camouflages around the bunker. She could hear voices drifting her way. She walked in the direction of the well but didn't see anyone yet.

Last of all, she checked that the booby trap was set. Fix wouldn't agree yet to her plan, but he had still built a trap, a great one, right outside the bunker in case of an attack. Cleo looked at the trap for a while before turning to go in.

She was about to take the usual steps to erase her footprints leading to the bunker when she paused. What would ever convince Fix that they couldn't keep hiding like this? It wouldn't work forever.

• • •

When Cleo came in, everyone jumped and then looked relieved. Todd and Rob had their arms around each other and around Gus. Nic was finishing her jobs plus Fix's. Fix hovered by her, but it was obvious his shoulder still hurt too much for him to do anything useful.

"Done," said Cleo briefly, going back to her corner. Nic nodded at her. Todd and Rob started to sing softly to Gus to distract him. Gus was better now, but he used to cry silently whenever they had to hide. Cleo knew how he felt—except she preferred to get mad.

Fix stood at the periscope. "I see them— just two, it looks like . . . They're heading straight for the well and pulling away all the brush we piled there . . . Like they knew where it was." He stopped, watching. "They're filling some bottles and stuff. Sitting down, drinking . . ."

Everyone held their breath until Gus's voice cut through the silence.

"What should we do now, Cleo? What are we going to do?"

"We're going to wait," Cleo laughed bitterly. "Like always . . ."

# CHAPTER ELEVEN

Fix stood at the periscope. He could hear the others murmuring behind him. He was glad Todd and Rob were there for Gus—he just didn't have it in him right now to be comforting. His shoulder still hurt a lot. But Cleo's words stung more. Why was she always spoiling for a fight these days?

Fix straightened up when he noticed movement through the periscope. The outside lens was scratched, but he could see two kids approaching. One had a shotgun over his shoulder. The other had his gun on a sling and was dragging it in the dirt behind him. In his free hand were two bottles of water.

"They're here."

The raiders were looking around suspiciously and glancing at the ground. Then they walked right toward the bunker—so close that Fix couldn't see them through the periscope anymore.

*Thump!* Everyone jumped, and Nic let out a little scream. But Fix couldn't take his eyes off of Cleo. She was on her feet, holding her gun. Her eyes were gleaming.

"Did you . . . Cleo, did you . . . ?" Fix couldn't say it.

Nic was there, pushing her herself between them. "They're at the door! They're going to break it down! What are we going to do?!"

Fix nudged her aside. "They can't break it down. It's too strong. But I saw them. I saw them. They walked right above here. They were looking . . . Cleo—"

*Thump!* Nic covered her mouth. Gus was crying.

Cleo interrupted Fix: "Did they have weapons?" Fix nodded. Cleo grinned. "Now, Fix. It's time. If the whole group comes here, they *will* be able to get in. We need to stop these two from getting back to their buddies and get their weapons. This is perfect. The trap is set. There's only two of them." The pounding on the door got louder. "We've talked about this possibility. Everyone knows what to do."

"But, Fix's shoulder . . ." Nic trailed off. She couldn't take it all in. She looked over at the ax in the corner.

"I'll do it," Todd said, standing up. Gus was in Rob's lap, but they both were looking up, ready. Cleo nodded. Todd grabbed the ax and a flare gun.

"Fix will be our spotter—he can help Nic get the bodies in," Cleo said. She looked at Rob. "You ready?" He nodded. Cleo knelt down in front of Gus. "Gus, everyone needs to help now. You need to start locking up all the food, okay?" Gus slid off Rob's lap and scurried over to the cupboards. Locking food away wasn't important, but Cleo felt like everyone needed a job.

"Where are they?" Nic whispered. "Do you think they went away?" Rob handed her the other flare gun.

Fix was at the periscope again. "They're pulling up a fence post," he said grimly.

"Okay, this is it," Cleo said. "Nic and Rob, get ready to throw the trap on my word, and then come out right behind me and Todd." She pushed Fix aside at the periscope. She was trembling with excitement.

# CHAPTER TWELVE

When Cleo had first discovered the flare guns stashed in the bunker, she was ecstatic. It was the first good thing they'd found at the farm as far as she was concerned. The flare guns were tucked away on a shelf, pistol grips out, so she'd thought they were real guns at first. She was disappointed when she saw what they actually were, but then she fired one of the flares into the side of the barn. When she saw the mark it made, she was sure the find was better than nothing.

The bunker only had two flare guns, but there were dozens of flares. It didn't take Fix long to figure out how to trigger them—a little spark from a battery set the guns off. The group had spent a day setting up two dozen flares so they'd go off simultaneously in the faces of anyone who tried to break down the door. The result would be more shock than injury, but Cleo was sure it would give their group time to fight back.

As usual, once Fix got going, he kept improving. An old tractor suspension spring was now rigged to throw the doors open a moment after the flares hit.

Cleo didn't take time to appreciate how well Fix's trap had worked as she darted up the stairs, gun ready. But the trap certainly worked well. The first kid, the one with his gun in a sling, was stunned. He reeled around a few feet from the door.

Cleo stayed in the shadow halfway up the stairs, giving her eyes time to adjust to the light. The kid—the boy—was young, younger than she was. He was perfectly framed for her in the door's opening. He was wild-looking, and she couldn't understand his gibberish as he clawed at his burning eyes. He was so young—

*Enough!* Cleo thought to herself. She raised her gun and stepped out of the shadows.

For a second, the kid froze and so did Cleo, as if having him in her sights connected the two of them. And for some reason, she felt like he should see her. In this moment, of all moments. As she stepped onto the top stair, the kid staggered back and fumbled with the sling on his shoulder.

He might have said, "No, please!" but she couldn't be sure. In that same moment, she fired and hit him squarely in the head.

The other one was more alert—or maybe seeing his companion killed snapped him to his senses. He dove for cover behind some logs. Cleo took her shot, but it hit a bit behind him.

The kid fired back and forced Cleo to dive away from the door. He quickly fired again. If Cleo had been watching from a distance, she would have been disgusted by the sloppy shots spraying at the bunker entrance. She was a few feet away from the door: far enough to be safe, but close enough to almost vomit as she saw Rob charge up the stairway—and into the line of fire.

As Rob screamed and fell back down the stairs, the kid took his chance. He dropped his shotgun and sprinted away from the bunker. Cleo took one look down the steps and then back at the fleeing kid. She felt the warrior's calm come over her. It really was like ice water.

The kid moved fast. He was looking over his shoulder and occasionally zigzagging, but he had more than a hundred yards to cross to get to the next cover. Cleo had no trouble getting a line on him in the open yard. He swerved a bit as she fired, though, and the shot clearly didn't kill him—at least not instantly like the other one. The kid wasn't going anywhere fast, but Cleo knew she couldn't afford to take a chance. She started across the yard toward the screaming boy. She grabbed his ancient, heavy shotgun on her way.

# CHAPTER THIRTEEN

"Cleo!" Fix shouted from the bottom of the stairs. He'd gone to check on her once they were sure Rob was going to be okay. The kid's gun had packed only bird shot, and the round had just grazed Rob's leg. Rob was bloody, but already protesting that he'd be fine.

When Cleo didn't answer, Fix made his way up the stairs to see her approaching the other kid. Fix started to run.

When he got to Cleo, he wished he hadn't.

He skidded to a halt in time to see her club the second kid to death with the butt of his rifle.

"You had another shot," he screamed. "God, Cleo, you could have finished it in a second."

"And if you think I'd waste ammo on him, you're nuts. Come on. Help me get the bodies into the bunker. Then we've got to cover our tracks back to the door. You can bet their buddies heard the shots." She was already pulling the dead kid by his feet. Fix wondered how they'd hide the bloody smear the kid was leaving. His head spun.

"Fix!" she yelled. "Snap out of it. We've got to move. Forget the other guy. I'll handle him. Just get the traps on the bunker reset. And tell the others—" She froze. "Rob! Fix, is he—"

Fix finally came around. "He's fine, Cleo. Just grazed him." He headed back to the bunker. "We'll reset the trap."

# CHAPTER FOURTEEN

"And fill me from the crown to the toe top-full of direst cruelty," Cleo whispered to herself. Two shotguns, and lots of ammunition clipped to the bandoliers the kids had strung over their shoulders! What fools those two had been to carry it all around with them. Sure, the ammo was just more birdshot, but that was way better than flares. *God, why didn't the second one take the time to reload instead of running?* she wondered. Then she remembered how young he had been, and his terror. Maybe somebody else had loaded the gun for him. Maybe he hadn't known how to reload it himself. She pushed the thought from her mind.

After Fix and Todd reset the traps, they and the others retreated to the far side of the bunker, away from the bodies. They picked at rations in silence while Cleo continued inspecting her haul. She could hardly wait to see what other goodies were on the bodies.

She started with the one who had been carrying the water. She flipped open his jacket and plunged her hands in his pockets. A knife! She hefted it in her hand. Might be a good one for throwing. She could practice later.

A little food in his pants pocket, but nothing else. She yanked off his boots and held one up. "Might be your size," she said to Todd, tossing them to him. He shrank back, and the boots clattered to the floor. Todd's pale face shone in the dim light. Rob had his arms around him. Cleo shrugged and turned back to the other body.

The second guy she'd killed had a few more shells in his coat pocket. Batteries in his pants pocket plus a small flashlight. *Nice*, thought Cleo. The coat looked warm, too. She struggled to pull it off his heavy body.

"Someone want to give me a hand?" Cleo called. No one responded. As she dragged the coat off, she could feel there was something in it. An inside pocket. A book!

Cleo sat back to flip through it. She'd savor it later, no matter what it was. But then she slowed down and started reading.

"Password: sanctuary . . . Refuge . . ." she murmured, squinting at the handwritten notes on the sides of the pages.

"What is it?" Nic finally asked.

Cleo glanced up, impatient. "Let me read. The rest of you could be getting all their clothes off. Once the bodies stiffen up, it'll be hard."

"That's disgusting," Nic said coldly. "You gonna pull their teeth out, too, Cleo, and make a necklace?"

"Everyone's always whining about not having any underwear. These guys have decent clothes. You don't want them? I'll wear them. But shut up so I can read."

No one moved, and Cleo went back to studying the book. She was quiet for a long time. When she looked up, her face beamed.

"This is pure gold," she said. "The book, or what's left of it, is some kind of survival guide. By some guy named Gene Matterhorn. A lot of pages are missing, so maybe they were just tearing it up to start fires or wipe their butts. But even better is what someone wrote in the margins of the pages.

"It's by someone called Ozymandias. He talks about a place called Refuge. It sounds like it's south of here—there are directions and maps. I guess it's pretty well defended. Sounds like there's a wall or something around it. But he gives the passwords for getting in, even tells a little what the place is like. The people, I mean . . ." Cleo trailed off, staring at the book. "Here, see for yourselves." Cleo tossed the book to Nic, who caught it automatically, and then started cleaning the guns, humming a little to herself.

# CHAPTER FIFTEEN

**N**ic slowly paged through the book. Fix's heart was pounding, and at the same time he felt numb. It was all too much, too fast. First all the violence and now this. Cleo finding another way to try to make them leave the farm. And he couldn't even read the stupid book for himself.

Nic glanced up at him and said, "I'll just read it out loud so we can all hear it, okay? Just the stuff about this place, Refuge. The survival stuff we can look at later."

When Nic finished, Fix's head hurt. He really needed to sleep or something before he could even think about this. But Nic had some questions.

"Why do you think this Ozymandias guy wrote all this stuff down? Doesn't sound very secure to me," Nic said to Cleo.

Cleo shrugged. "He must have been passing the information to other people like the ones in Refuge. Strength in numbers. He's putting together an army, maybe. Of civilized people. People who can rea—" She stopped herself.

"Or maybe his people are the ones over there. The ones you just enjoyed killing!" Nic said, her voice shaking

"Look at the book," Cleo said. "You can see those idiots were ripping it apart. Do you think they could read? They're different from us, Nic, and you know it. Look at how they tried to break in here. We wouldn't have done that."

"No, you would have just waited 'til we came out and killed us and then taken everything if you had been those guys. Being smarter doesn't make you better, Cleo." Nic sounded sad.

Cleo shook her head. "That's crazy. I've only ever defended us. Kept us safe." She looked over at Fix. "This is a waste of time. The important thing is, what are we going to do next?"

Everyone started to talk at once. Fix put his head in his hands, trying to block them all out, to think his own thoughts. Finally Nic said, "Fix? What do you think?"

"I think," he said slowly, "that it *is* weird that all this stuff is written down. I mean, it's not just because I can't . . . read," he said in a low voice. "I can keep a lot of stuff in my head, and so can all of you. If someone wanted to tell you something so important, why wouldn't you just remember it? I think it could be a trap."

"But why?" Rob asked. "Why would these people at Refuge try to, like, what, lure people in? Why wouldn't they just want to be left alone if they didn't want new people?"

"Well, maybe they're trying to get people's stuff too," Fix started, not looking at Cleo.

"But they could do that a lot easier by just attacking people as they came near the town. Like Cleo said, those guys and a lot of others who've gotten to be like animals don't bother with reading. Seems to me like it has to be a secret message," Todd said.

"Maybe Ozymandias was captured or something," Rob added. "Knew he was toast. So he wrote this down, just in case someone found it."

Rob and Todd were still holding hands. Fix had never realized how much they wanted to leave the farm. He'd thought they were on his side.

"Well, they're not all stupid," Fix said. "Maybe by now the nomad kids have taken over Refuge and we'd just be going into more danger. This is the safest place we've found." He felt like he was pleading with them.

"Maybe we should vote," Cleo said. "All in favor of going to Refuge?" Cleo, Rob, and Todd all raised their hands. After a moment,

Nic did too. Gus looked back and forth between everyone and burst into tears. Fix wished he could cry too.

# CHAPTER SIXTEEN

"**I** know it's not what you want, Fix," Cleo said, trying to sound gentle. "But we've always run things by vote. I hope we can still count on you." After a long pause, Fix nodded his head. But he still wouldn't look at her.

It took them almost a week to get ready to leave. The biggest problem was fuel for the truck. But Fix pitched in. Even Cleo was impressed when he managed to get the truck to start using some sludgy old frying oil he'd found next to a busted state-fair food cart in the barn. It took him days of tireless work, but soon Fix reported that he would have enough fuel to get them over a few miles of hills.

"It won't be fast, but it'll probably smell good," he had said. It was as close to a joke as Fix ever offered.

Fix didn't talk much to Cleo as the group worked, checking off lists. Cleo acted like she didn't notice, like they were all just busy getting ready to go as soon as possible.

The first night after the vote, Cleo asked Todd instead of Fix to help her bury the bodies. She stayed out of Fix's way, so it wouldn't be so obvious to the others that he was mad at her. It helped that they were all keeping busy, gathering supplies and trying to figure out what they'd have to leave behind.

Cleo was more focused on the farm's defenses than on preparing to leave. She had a bad feeling that more raiders could come while the group was busy with other stuff. Nic and the others could pack everything up. Cleo wanted to set up some traps and keep watch. But some nights, when she woke up and heard everyone breathing around her, she'd crawl over to Fix and sit next to him while he slept. She missed him. And she needed a way to be friends with him again—she wanted his help with the big traps.

Four days after she'd killed the intruders, Cleo hit on the right plan.

"Fix," she said casually as they were all eating. "I think before we go we should work some more on reading. You were starting to get it before we left Minneapolis, so I know you can do it." She tried to look unconcerned—like it would be no big deal.

"Too busy," Fix grunted, shoving food in his mouth.

Nic looked from Cleo to Fix. Nic could read too. Not as well as Cleo, but better than Fix. Cleo could tell she knew what was up. She didn't care.

"We'll find time," Cleo said. "It could be really important. We'll need all the help we can get once we start traveling. I think we might be ready to leave pretty soon." She stared at Fix, willing him to look at her. Slowly he did, losing the stony look on his face.

"Okay." He shrugged. "We'll see."

Cleo cornered him later that evening. She had the survival guide. "It's still light enough to see," she said briskly. "Let's sit over here."

They sat down in the grass together. Fix still looked unwilling. Together they watched as a bird skimmed overhead, flying home for the night.

"Nice out tonight, huh?" Cleo said, wanting a little friendliness. Fix looked around the farm as though he was seeing it for the first time.

"It's beautiful," he said, more to himself. For the first time, Cleo saw what the farm meant to him and felt bad. But she took a big breath and plowed on—she didn't regret winning the vote.

"Okay, you know the letters and their sounds, right? So now let's look at how they make words." She flipped open the book and found some simple words. "See? B-I-G. Big."

They kept going like that for a while. Fix was sounding out the words and sentences, but he seemed bored. Plus, Cleo thought he was just making lucky guesses in some places because he already knew a lot of stuff in the survival guide by instinct. Half the time Fix didn't seem to be even looking at the words. They needed something better.

"Hey, Fix, you're doing really well. I think you're ready for something harder. I mean, better," she said brightly. "Let me get my book."

Fix tilted his head toward the sunset. "It's getting dark."

Cleo was already on her feet. "Just a little more. I'll be right back." She dashed into the bunker and dropped down next to him again a moment later. She was excited to share her book with Fix. She didn't understand it herself, but she knew it was full of power.

"Here, this part is in the *Hamlet* section. It makes me think of my dad, or of you sometimes," Cleo said without looking at Fix. "Try it."

"What a . . . pies?" Fix started.

"*Piece*," Cleo said. "See the e on the end?"

"What a piece of work is a man," Fix read slowly. "How noble in rea, rea, rea-son, how in—this is too hard, Clee."

"No, you're doing great. Just break it down, like it's a machine, Fix. Words have parts too. Once you know how to put them together, you can make anything."

"In-fin . . . ite? What's that?"

"*Infinite*. It means, like, forever, or it never ends. Here, that word is like, *faculties*, but I don't know exactly what that means," Cleo confessed. "It's the next part I like."

"In form and moving how ex-press and ad, admir . . . able." Fix sighed in frustration.

Cleo leaned over his shoulder and read softly, "In action, how like an angel. In apprehension, how like a god. The beauty of the world. The paragon of animals!"

She stopped, and they were quiet for a moment.

"That made you think of me?" Fix asked.

Cleo nodded, looking down.

"Thanks," Fix said and leaned into her a little. He was quiet for a while. "Clee."

"Yeah?"

"What's an angel?"

It was her turn to be quiet. "I'm not really sure, Fix."

# CHAPTER SEVENTEEN

Fix's shoulder was healed enough that he was able to load the last of the heavy supply boxes onto the truck. Everything was pretty much ready. Cleo had suggested they leave that day. Fix hadn't exactly agreed, but it looked now like they'd be heading out. He was standing in the truck bed, having just placed the last box, when he saw the gang of six coming down the hillside.

"Clee! They're coming. Everybody get ready! Remember what Cleo showed you!"

Fix had to marvel at how well Cleo had drilled everyone. How tight her plan was and how carefully everyone followed it. It had seemed silly to Fix how she'd made everyone do drills two days ago. But now, seeing everyone moving quickly and calmly, it didn't seem silly at all.

Cleo had pointed out that they'd be sitting ducks if they spent all their time packing supplies and fixing the truck. Once Fix had solved the fuel problem, Cleo had gathered everybody together and they'd planned for the next wave of nomads to show up. Now they'd see how well the plan worked. Fix wasn't even as worried as he'd thought he'd be.

• • •

Nic, Gus, and Todd got into the truck. They had one shotgun and the two flare guns. The truck was parked so that once the raiders started for the well, Nic, Gus, and Todd could start firing and drive the raiders toward the only cover: the windmill control shed.

Fix took his position inside the control shed. After Cleo had talked to him about making traps, while he was combing through the shed in search of tools to take south, Fix realized that the mistake that had wrecked the generator linkage and messed up his shoulder was also the beginning of a decent trap.

He had stood in the yard for half an hour before Cleo came up to him and asked what he was daydreaming about. When he'd told her, her eyes had sparkled. Between the two of them, it had only taken another half hour to sketch out how the trap would work.

As the gang of nomads approached, at least one thing was on Fix and Cleo's side. The wind was blowing hard out of the north, and the windmill was turning beautifully.

# CHAPTER EIGHTEEN

Cleo and Rob were hidden behind the oil barrels. The gang had just entered the yard.

Cleo looked into Rob's eyes. "You've got to wait to shoot until you know you've got a kill. Understand? You've only got two rounds." Cleo's whole body felt like a drawn bow.

Rob nodded and clicked off the safety. Flares burst from the truck, and kids screamed. "I'm ready," he said without emotion. "Let's do this."

The gun clicked as he pumped a cartridge into the chamber. They had to make sure the kids headed for the control shed and toward Fix's trap.

Cleo stood up and started to scream, "Hey, you—" when a shotgun blast drowned her out. The shot was off its mark, but neither Rob nor Cleo needed another warning. They tore off toward the windmill, hoping Fix had everything ready.

They were ten yards from the windmill when the next shot echoed over their heads. Rob was first to bang through the doorway, yelling, "They're coming," with Cleo on his heels.

"Now or never, Fix!" Cleo screamed.

Fix pointed to the back door and to Rob and Cleo. "Get going," he said. Then he snuffed the lantern. The room was dark except for the light pouring through the open front door.

Rob headed out the back door as Fix began pulling a huge lever he'd made from old black gas pipe. The gears ground and screamed as the nomad kids banged into the control house. All six were inside.

For a moment, Cleo could only hear the raiders' breathing as they strained to see anything in the dark room. Then she heard Fix: "Come on!"

He was straining, she could see in the gloom, to pull the lever the final few inches. It was stuck. He caught Cleo's eye and she knew in an instant.

Cleo stepped into the light, firing her last shot into the six kids. One fell. She took another step back inside and was nearly to Fix when the first of their shots hit. She twisted and screamed but made it to Fix's post. He started to let go of the lever and reach for her. Another shot ricocheted over their heads as Fix felt Cleo add her weight to his own, and the lever fell the rest of the way forward.

# CHAPTER NINETEEN

Cleo's chest felt like it had sprung a leak. The sound of a chain winding filled the control shed, and the front door slammed closed. One of the kids fired another shot. And then another. And then Fix and Rob were lifting her up. And then they were through the door and into the light of day. Someone slammed the door behind her and barred it shut as the sounds of gears clashing and metal twisting echoed through the valley.

Moments later they were all in the truck. Rob and Fix were still beside Cleo, breathing hard. She saw the shadow of the windmill. And then the shadow moved and the metal noise grew unbearable and the shadow was gone. And then silence.

# CHAPTER TWENTY

Fix was barely aware of what he did or what he saw in those moments after leaving the control shed. There was so much blood. Cleo's blood. And the sound of the windmill ripping itself apart.

The idea to bring down the windmill had come to Fix when he felt a twinge in his shoulder and remembered trying to fix the generator connection alone. He had remembered the power of that windmill. He, Rob, Todd, and Cleo had spent an afternoon connecting two hundred feet of steel cable to the windmill's shaft, then weaving it through support beams inside the tower.

Fix couldn't help himself. As the sound of crumpling aluminum echoed through the low hills, he looked over his shoulder. He stumbled, bringing down Rob and Cleo with him. They all watched as the windmill fell, the length of cable wrapping around the shaft, pulling the tower into itself—and everyone stuck inside.

Rob got back to his feet and dragged Cleo the last few steps to the truck. "Come on, Fix. Don't let up. We've almost got her to the truck," Rob said through gritted teeth.

The truck. That was the only thing now. They were really leaving. No turning back.

• • •

Todd gunned the engine, and the bed of the pickup vibrated as they rumbled down the gravel driveway. Cleo couldn't see over the edge of the bed, but part of the bottom was rusted out and she could watch the road beneath them. They were moving, really moving.

Moving was great, and Cleo smiled. The smile didn't last because breathing was getting harder. She turned to look up at Fix.

Fix was pressing a bundle of shirts and rags and whatever into her chest. Maybe that's why she couldn't breathe. *If only Fix would stop pushing on my chest*, she thought. Then she coughed. The taste of blood was unmistakable. Fix's pushing wasn't the problem. It also wouldn't be the solution. The past ten minutes were coming back to her.

Fix was covered in blood, and his face was frantic. He seemed to Cleo to be whispering to himself. She tried to focus on his lips. *Focus. Fix, why don't you talk louder? There's so much wind up where you are.* She fought to catch his eyes. *There.*

She finally made out his whispering: "Come on, Cleo. Come on." Or maybe he was screaming. "Stay with us, Cleo. Please."

She raised her left hand near his face. The right arm didn't seem to work. "Fix." Her voice was faint. He didn't hear. She managed to get her left hand to his mouth. Left arm didn't seem much better. There. *Nice lips.*

"Fix."

Fix had been looking everywhere but Cleo's eyes. He turned to face her. "Cleo. I'm trying everything. Just hold on. Please. I can—"

"Fix me?" she whispered. "Fix." She shook her head and touched his face again. Nice cheek. "The book—the map. Ozymandias. Refuge, Fix. They're real. I know they are. Get the others there. I know you can."

"I'll get us all there, Cleo. All of us. Just hold on. I can stop the bleeding. You're going to—"

She coughed and gagged. More blood. "Read to me, Fix. Come down here with me, Fix. Out of the wind. It's quiet, Fix. You can read to me." She dislodged the book from the pocket of her too-big coat. "It's *Hamlet.* I thought we could practice on the road. So important. So important now that you learn."

Fix took the book from her. The page was familiar, and he was thankful. He began. "What—what a piece of—"

She touched his face again and he stopped. "Down here with me, Fix. So I can hear you. Hear you read."

Fix stretched out next to Cleo, his mouth at the level of her ear. She stared up at the impossibly blue sky. She listened hard.

Fix took a deep breath, and read: "What a piece of work is—is a woman, how noble in reason, how infinite in faculties, in form and moving how express and admirable, in action how like an angel, in apprehension how like a god! The beauty of the world, the paragon of animals—and yet. . . ."

# CHAPTER TWENTY-ONE

Fix could tell his shoulder was healed because it didn't hurt at all as he dug. Thoughts like that, stupid thoughts, floated through his head as he pushed the shovel deeper and deeper. He wished his shoulder did hurt. He wanted pain to drown out the stupid thoughts.

Todd and Rob were trying to help, but Fix wouldn't give up the shovel. There wasn't really enough room in the hole, either, for more than one person to dig at once. Fix made the dirt fly. He began to sweat, and he could feel some pain in his hands. Finally.

*How deep?* he wondered. And then he wished that he could just dig forever, infinite, as Cleo had taught him. He never wanted to stop and have to look up to see all of them, with her missing.

Cleo would have known how deep it should be.

Todd and Rob tried again to get him to stop. Fix just choked back a grim laugh and shook his head. He kept digging. They went away.

"Fix? Fix! Fix, stop, that's enough. It's plenty deep, Fix. Stop." Nic's voice broke on the last word. She crouched down so her face was level with Fix's.

He paused, forced to look at her. Her face was streaked with tears. He wondered if his was too.

"This is good, Fix. You did a good job. I have her ready. You know we can't stop here, and it's getting dark." Nic held out her hand to Fix. He took it and climbed out of the grave.

Now the moment he dreaded. He saw Gus, his lips pressed together, clutching a handful of weeds and wildflowers. Todd and Rob standing next to Gus, looking at the body. The truck, dark against the sunset. And the sight Fix couldn't avoid. Cleo, lying on the ground. No bloody holes—where had they gone? Her jacket and book were off to one side.

"I cleaned her up," Nic said. "I don't care about our water supply, I used some. I changed her shirt. I wanted her to look . . . right."

Fix glanced at Nic and saw that she was shivering a little in the wind. She still had on her sweater, but she'd given Cleo the shirt she always wore underneath it.

Fix nodded, his jaw clenched. Nic turned to Todd and Rob. They moved forward to pick Cleo up.

"Wait," Fix croaked. "What about her jacket? And book?"

"Those are for you, Fix," said Nic gently. "I think she'd want you to have them." Nic walked over and picked up the jacket and coverless book and handed them to Fix.

Cleo would be cold without the jacket. The dirt he had dug felt cold. *But she's dead*, said a voice in his head. *Take what you need. Things are for the living.* It was Cleo's voice, and Fix felt a crazy need to laugh again.

He felt Nic shiver a bit again next to him. "Here," he said, thrusting the jacket at her. "You take it. You need it. Cleo liked things . . . things that were needed." Nic put on the jacket. It had been large on Cleo and was even bigger on her.

Fix gripped the book tightly and nodded at Todd and Rob. They lifted Cleo with ease. It seemed to Fix she should be heavier. Cleo had always seemed so full of things. Plans, energy, words, and sometimes hate. Love, too. He knew that now.

Todd and Rob had an awkward time getting Cleo in the grave, but they were very gentle lowering her down. Again Fix thought that Cleo would have known, would have read somewhere, about the best way to move a body into a grave. Or she would say it didn't matter. But it did. Todd arranged Cleo the best he could and climbed out.

Nic motioned to Gus. He gave everyone a flower and threw the rest into the grave.

Nic cleared her throat. "Cleo, you always did your best to keep us safe. You took care of us. I— I'll—" She clamped her mouth closed and blinked her eyes. The others waited for her to continue, but she shook her head desperately. Then she dropped her flower in the grave. She looked back at the others.

Rob stepped forward. "Cleo, you were tough when we couldn't be. You helped us to be strong." He dropped his flower in.

Todd's face was like Nic's. He was trying to hold back tears. All of his muscles were twitching. "You were always yourself, Cleo," he said as he let go of his flower.

Gus stared at his empty hands and then glanced around wildly. The others waited while he ran to pick a dandelion gone halfway to seed. He came back panting. "I wish you weren't dead, Cleo," he said. As he dropped in the dandelion, some of the seeds floated off and into the grass.

Everyone looked at Fix.

"We love you," he whispered. His voice didn't seem to work. "And you love us." He stopped. He tried to make his voice stronger, but he only wanted to talk to Cleo, anyway. It didn't matter if the others could hear. "We'll get there, Cleo, I swear it. I'll get them there." He dropped his flower and watched it land near Cleo's hip.

Fix looked away as soil began to fall on Cleo's feet. Rob had the shovel and was scooping dirt in from the pile Fix had made.

"Can't we cover her first? I don't want . . ." he trailed off. Cleo wouldn't waste a blanket on a dead body. *Are you crazy?!* he heard her say. He looked at Nic. She smiled at him sadly. She was thinking the same thing.

"I'm sorry, Cleo," Fix whispered. He stepped closer to the pile and started pushing armfuls of dirt into her grave. He didn't look where they landed. A moment later, everyone was pushing dirt with their hands. Soon the grave was almost full. Rob motioned everyone back as he took the shovel and smoothed the dirt carefully.

"We need to camouflage it," Fix announced. "I don't want anyone . . ." He noticed the others, covered in dirt, except where tears or snot had made tracks down their faces. Everyone was looking to him. "Maybe only Cleo would be smart enough to look for stuff on dead bodies," he said. Smiles flickered for a moment. "But I don't want her grave messed with. Let's get some branches and dried grass and leaves. Then we need to go."

As Fix got behind the steering wheel, he looked once more through the side mirror toward Cleo's grave. Rob got in next to him and opened the survival book to the map of Refuge. Nic and Todd raised the sail in the truck bed. Fix felt the sail fill, and the truck began to move. South, with the wind.

# ABOUT THE AUTHOR

Elias Carr is a writer and editor who survives in
St. Paul, Minnesota.

The world is
over.

AFTER THE DUST SETTLED

Can you
survive
what's next?

# AFTER THE DUST SETTLED

### Fight the Wind

Fix has a gift for machines. If he can fix up an old wind turbine, he and his friends will be able to live at their Iowa camp for as long as they want. Cleo says no way. She'd rather try to find a city that's rumored to be growing in the southwest. But if another rumor is true—that raiders are heading toward the camp—the only real choice will be fight or die.

### Pig City

Malik and his friends try to avoid cities, but they look for shelter in downtown Des Moines once a winter storm hits. They're quickly trapped in the middle of a struggle between the city's two biggest gangs: the peaceful members of the Coalition and the forces of Pig City, who want to turn everyone else into hog food.

### Plague Riders

When Shep's parents disappeared, he agreed to deliver medicine for the sinister Doctor St. John. The doctor runs the camp of River's Edge with total control, but the pills he makes are the only defense against the nightpox plague. On one trip, Shep learns that his parents may still be alive. With fellow rider Cara by his side, he prepares to escape from River's Edge.

### River Run

Freya and her sister have spent years as captives in a Minneapolis basement. After her sister disappears, Freya decides to break out—and finds herself heading down the Mississippi River with a strange young boy. Are the boy's sunny stories about Norlins true? Or will the end of Freya's journey be the most dangerous part?

### Shot Down

Malik and the Captain, a gruff inventor, are on a hot air balloon tour of apocalyptic America—until a bullet sends their ride to the ground. A crash landing is just the beginning of their troubles, as the two travelers discover a family that hunts people for sport and begin a run for their lives across the hills and fields of Kentucky.

### Snakebite

Beckley's crew has made its way from Montana to South Dakota, living off the land and staying out of trouble. But trouble soon finds them. First, a snake sinks its fangs into the moody Hector. Then a clan of savage kids runs off with Beckley's sister. Will the group's survival knowledge be enough to get her back?

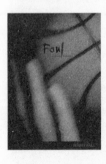